Scandalous Series

Because of Devon

By Willa Winters

Table of Contents

SYNOPSIS

Sometimes the best laid plans backfire.

My name is Taylor. I'm eighteen, and I live a rich life. My mother died when I was young, and my wealthy stepfather who came into my life when I was only two, has raised me as his own.

Here's the problem. Devon is so over-protective and his strict rules and curfews are driving me nuts! I have no social life whatsoever!

But, I have a plan.

Maybe Devon needs a distraction so I set about providing one for him in hopes that he'll lay off with all his restrictions with me. So, I fix him up with my favorite teacher – who I'm hoping will also give me a better grade this last semester.

But when Ms. Henderson shows up to our house for dinner, all my plans go kind of . . . off-track! Oy! Some things are just too difficult to predict!

Adult Content

CHAPTER 1

"Sometimes I hate my life," I griped to my best friend Shelly as we sat at the Pizza Barn, stuffing our faces with pepperoni pizza and guzzling sodas.

She looked over at me, wiping some pizza sauce from her lips with a napkin, "Why do you hate your life?" she asked frowning, "You've got it way better than me for shit's sake."

"How do you figure?" I challenged.

"Well, have you forgotten about that totally cool car your stepdad bought you for your eighteenth birthday, Taylor?" Her eyes were bugging out at me which was a sure sign she thought I was totally clueless. I knew that would be her comeback.

"Big deal," I replied dryly. "So he bought me a new car."

"Not just *any* new car, Taylor. He bought you a fucking Mercedes SLC for Chrissake!"

My best friend obviously was missing the point.

"Okay, so Shelly, what is so great about having a car when he gives me a curfew that *might* be appropriate for a thirteen year old? I'm fucking eighteen years old and he still treats me as if I'm a child. Home at eleven? Puhleeze."

She grabbed another slice of pizza shrugging, "Well I think you have a great stepdad. He's pretty cool, not to mention how freaking hot he is."

She fanned herself with a hand as if to drive home the point that yes, my stepfather at thirty-eight was a gorgeous male specimen. What good did that do me when he was so damn strict and protective?

"Shelly, he still has parental controls put on my damn laptop! He simply doesn't get that I'm not ten years old anymore. If Mom were still here, she would never be that strict and overbearing with me that's for sure.

My friend's face went solemn. She had never been faced with the death of a parent, let alone two. My father had died three months before I was born in a freak car accident.

My mother had married Devon Wilkes, a high-powered venture capitalist she met when she worked as a receptionist at his firm when I was just a year and a half old. He was as they say, the only father I'd ever really known.

Devon Wilkes was beyond wealthy. He was, as my grandmother termed it, filthy rich. I'd never wanted for anything. Nor had my mother.

He'd treated her like a queen, and me as his princess, taking us on lavish vacations, expensive cruises, and a home that was the best in town complete with a swimming pool, tennis court, and hot tub.

We had people who cooked and cleaned for us, but sadly, Devon was gone a lot traveling in his business to faraway places.

When Mom developed breast cancer when I was only eleven. Devon sent her to the best surgeons, oncologists, and hospitals clear on the other side of the country to make sure she would get well.

Sadly, she hadn't.

She died when I was fourteen. I was lost without her. But the thought of moving to my grandmother's home, ten hours away from where I'd been raised was never an option.

"I promised your mother that I'd raise you Taylor, you're my daughter in every sense of the word, I won't let you go."

Those words had comforted me and it'd never been an issue until I hit sixteen. It was as if my dad didn't know who I really was! His constant monitoring me of any social activities was damn near suffocating.

We faced off in too many battles to count, and despite the fact I'd turned eighteen four months ago didn't mean squat to him because he still refused to consider me anything more than a child! It was infuriating.

I was a senior in the private high school I attended at his insistence. He thought it was better than the public school systems.

My grades weren't half bad, and I'd made the varsity cheerleading squad which took a whole helluva lot of time and commitment another thing he just didn't seem to understand.

Shelly interrupted my thoughts. "Hey, does your dad date anybody, Taylor? Maybe he just needs to, you know, let off some steam?"

I was thoughtful as I considered her words. He'd never brought a woman around since Mom had passed, but I'd be truly naive to think he hadn't been involved with anyone. Still, maybe I could be of some assistance in that endeavor.

"Shelly, you are brilliant!" I replied, slurping up the rest of my soda, "You've given me the best idea ever!"

She peered over her glasses at me, her brows furrowed. "What do you mean?"

"Ms. Henderson, our English teacher. Recently divorced, hot as all get out, she would be perfect for Dad!" I exclaimed. "Plus the bitch is threatening to fail me this quarter. Can you imagine what further restrictions I'll have if that happens? Maybe I'll suck up to her and ask her over to dinner with the excuse I need some tutoring. It's a win-win! She'll see just how dedicated I am to turning my grades around, and if I'm lucky, she and Dad will click and both of them will be off of my back. Perfect idea, thank you!"

"Oh jeez Taylor, I did all that?"

I gave her a huge grin. "You planted the seed, now it's up to me to bring it to harvest. If Dad has somebody--even if it's just a sexual distraction for a while, he'll let up on all those stupid rules and regulations he dishes out to me. And if he slides the big one to Henderson, I just make get an "A" this quarter without doing squat myself. It's perfect, can't you see that?"

She shrugged, getting up from her chair. "If you say so," she replied, "C'mon, we need to jet if you're going to make it home before curfew."

I glanced at the clock. Shit she was right. "I hear that. I'm not up for another grounding because I walked in ten minutes late for shit's sake."

I dropped Shelly off and then made fast tracks to our place which bordered a small lake. As I pressed the button to open the iron gates, I glanced at the digital clock on the dash. Five minutes to spare. And it was a weekend night. This shit had to go I thought to myself. And on

Monday, with any luck, I could start the ball rolling with Dad and Ms. Henderson.

As soon as I stepped inside the marble foyer, Dad was coming down the winding staircase in his smoking jacket, a crystal glass with a couple of ice cubes and two fingers of Scotch in his hand.

He was a creature of habit. I would've been surprised had he not been doing exactly that. It was his eleven p.m. Taylor check.

"Did you have a nice time at the game?'" he asked.

I tossed my pom-poms on the round table in the foyer and shrugged. "We won 72 to 60. The after game sucked donkey balls," I griped.

His brow furrowed in confusion. "After game? What was the after game?" he questioned.

I started up the staircase brushing past his tall, muscular frame. "Well, Dad, for most of the seniors it's going back to somebody's house to celebrate a victory. For me, it's slopping down some pizza and soda with Shelly and having to be home by eleven so you're not calling out the National Guard," I snipped.

He grabbed my arm as I tried to pass him. "Now listen, Taylor," he said in his calm, fatherly tone, "There's no reason you can't go to the after game parties as long as it's chaperoned, there's no alcohol or drugs, you're not canoodling with some horny teenage boy and you're home by eleven."

He dropped my arm, his eyes still focused on me. I gave him an eye roll and then continued up the carpeted stairs.

"Seriously, Dad," I mumbled, "What would actually be the point of my going then? To be the token nerd?"

He sighed and called up after me. "There's absolutely nothing wrong or shameful about preserving your virtue and exercising good sense. Your mother was a prime example of that, even when I met her and she was in her mid-twenties. A fine respectable woman, and I am trying my best to parent you as I know she would want. Someday you'll appreciate my effort."

"Doubtful," I grumbled under my breath, slamming my bedroom door behind me.

God, he so needed to get laid. I was almost looking forward to school on Monday so I could start the sexual wheels of my plan of hooking him up with Ms. Henderson.

CHAPTER 2

It was Monday morning and I'd never been more excited to get to school. Imagine that? As I drug myself out of bed, I went to my walk-in closet, peeling off my pajamas, and rooted through the racks, looking for one of my plain, pleated uniform skirts which was required by the school.

Shit, they'd all been laundered by Berta on Friday before she left. I recalled her bitching at me that she'd had to search the floor of my room, under the bed, and in my bathroom hamper to gather them all up to wash. Undoubtedly, they were hanging in the laundry room as they required drip dry.

I jumped in the shower, and once finished, I'd hurriedly donned panties and a bra, making a mad dash downstairs to retrieve one of them.

Just as I was heading back upstairs, I passed Dad coming down, impeccably dressed in one of his Armani suits. He stopped short on the stairway, his gaze taking full inventory. His faced reddened as his hand shot up to loosen his tie a bit around the neck.

"Taylor," he chastised, "Don't you a have robe to put on instead of prancing around the house in your underwear?"

I saw his Adams' apple bobbing and a frown made an appearance across his handsome face.

My brow knitted in confusion.

I glanced down at my body. All the vital parts were covered were they not? I looked back up at him still not quite understanding his fussiness about seeing me in my underwear. "Dad," I said with a laugh, "You used to change my diapers, remember?"

He seemed to be choking on his tie, still jerking at it as if it was cutting off his windpipe.

"Damn, Taylor! You're long out of diapers. You're a full grown woman and it's not appropriate for you to be prancing around here half-naked! What if one of the staff were here? Or if I happened to be entertaining a business client?"

"Huh," I replied, still a bit dumbfounded, "Okay, it's seven a.m. on a Monday morning. There's no staff in yet, and I hardly think you'd have a business associate in here this early. You need to chill. Maybe you simply need to get laid, have you ever considered that?"

I'd never in my life said anything like that to him, and I immediately knew it might not have been the smartest thing to do.

I saw his face flush with anger I presumed, and his cheek twitched which was a totally new thing for me. God, I must've really pissed him off!

In a nanosecond, I felt his grip underneath my elbow as he snatched me up, and immediately we were face to face - within inches.

"You need to watch your mouth, Taylor! I am your father, maybe not by blood, but I sure as hell haven't raised you to speak so disrespectfully, or conduct yourself in such a crude manner. I am the *parent* here, and you damn well will remember that in the future. Now, if I say you need to dress more appropriately when you come out of your room, then that's what you damn well will do!"

With that, he gave me a swift smack on the ass, releasing me and then turning his back so that I had no opportunity to respond. I watched in awe as he continued downstairs to the main hall and then took the wing which led to the kitchen.

I was dumbfounded. No, that wasn't quite right. I was shocked. Not so much because of the harmless swat he'd given my ass, but the fact that I had actually enjoyed him going all alpha parental on me. My thighs clenched as I relived it a few times before I finally made my way back to my room.

I'd never thought of Devon as a sexual being, but surely, he'd had some action since Mom passed. He'd never brought anyone around, but then again, he traveled an awful lot, worked long hours even when he was in town, so I'm sure opportunities presented themselves in abundance.

I made a mental note to scour his suite once I got home from school this afternoon. He never made it home before dinner at seven, so I'd have plenty of time. I was surprised I hadn't thought of it before.

CHAPTER 3

It had worked like a charm at school. Ms. Henderson was a bit taken aback by my invitation, but I somehow used my acting skills to convince her I really needed some help on the upcoming term paper.

When I slipped in a bit of a lie in there when I told her my dad really wanted to meet her. That had definitely sparked her interest. She'd seen my dad a few times at the football games he'd made it to in order to watch my cheerleading skills.

I informed Berta, our housekeeper, as soon as I got home from school, that we would be having a guest for dinner the following evening. She gave me a look that clearly said *What the hell are you up to now?* But I wasn't about to clue her in on my plan.

Upstairs, I crept down the hallway to Dad's suite. The double doors were closed, as always, but that didn't stop me from Operation Snoop on Devon.

An hour later, I was sorely disappointed.

Nothing.

No porn, no videos, not even a box of condoms. I was just about ready to call it a total failure when an old hatbox of Mom's sitting on a shelf in his walk-in closet caught my eye. It surprised me that he still had any of her belongings around. He'd donated everything of hers to Vincent DePaul shortly after she passed.

I stood on my tip toes my hand working to move it closer to the edge, when it tumbled and fell to the carpeted floor, the contents spilling from it. There were a bunch of photographs.

And silk panties.

I knelt down to and picked up one of the photos. My God! It was a picture of me! And not some baby or childhood picture, it was recent!

I was in my shower, start naked. I quickly sorted through the rest. They were ALL pictures of me in some form of undress. But when? How?

Did Dad have hidden cameras on me?

And then I inspected the panties. They were silk thong panties, just like the ones I wore. I had dozens of them; too many to miss a few, but I picked up a black one, and for some odd reason, held it up to my nose and gave the crotch a sniff.

Eww! I could smell the scent of my pussy on the silky material. These were *mine*!

Why would he grab several of my soiled panties to keep hidden away in his closet?

And then I knew why. It was as plain as day to me. Devon Wilkes, my dad for all intents and purposes, lusted for me.

It all made sense now: his strict curfews, his overly protective rules for me. His total inflexibility with respect to the boys who'd asked me out. Yeah, I was allowed to date, but with those restrictive curfews, along with the fact he had GPS tracking on my phone and my car, I mean, shit, no wonder I was still a virgin at eighteen!

Maybe it was time I fixed his wagon. He had, after all, invaded my privacy in the most intimate and inappropriate ways.

I quickly put everything back in his closet and went to my suite, grabbing my cell phone off of the dresser.

"Shelly," I said as soon as she answered, "Can your brother get me some of that Liquid-X you told me about?"

There was a silent pause, and then of course, I got the usual third degree from my best friend. I clued her in on my plan, and while she was horrified at what I'd discovered in Dad's closet, she cautioned me on taking my revenge that far.

"No lectures," I argued, "I'm doing this. Can your brother hook me up? I'll need it tomorrow."

"Oh geez," she relented, "The things I do for you, Taylor. Consider it done, but keep me out of it after that, got it?"

"No probs, love you!"

As I snuggled down under the covers to go to sleep, I was content with the knowledge that my dad was going to have the time of his life when he met Mrs. Henderson.

CHAPTER 4

The dinner table was set. I'd done it myself, making sure our best crystal and silver were laid out, complete with linen tablecloth and napkins.

"I don't know what you're up to, Taylor, but whatever it is, you sure are putting a lot of effort into it," Berta remarked as she pulled the roasted chicken out of the oven. "I'm glad I'm out of here once this dinner is ready."

"Relax, Berta," I said with a laugh. "I'm just playing a little matchmaker with Dad. It's all good."

"Uh huh," she muttered, not bothering to hide her skepticism. "Good luck with that. Does your father know that's was this is about?"

"I don't want to be that *obvious*, Berta," I remarked. "He knows one of my teachers is coming to dinner and he's fine with that. I'll simply let nature take its course."

***

At exactly seven-fifteen, Dad, Ms. Henderson and I sat down to break bread. I'd personally filled their wine goblets, putting a few drops of the Liquid-X into each of them.

I could tell Ms. Henderson was in awe of Devon, as they talked about some of their common interests. I sat there in silence, praying one of them would be some random fucking. We were on dessert when it finally hit them.

Oh my God!

I knew the effects of Liquid-X, and mixed with four glasses of Chardonnay, I could only hope at some point I'd know when it had kicked in. I was now seeing the signs.

Their eyes were glazed; they were studying one another as if they were two primal animals with nothing on their mind but mating. That was my signal.

"Listen," I said, getting up from the table, "I'm going to clear the dishes if you guys want to take another glass of wine into the living room so we can all chat?"

"Sounds good," my dad slurred, not taking his eyes off of Ms. Henderson. They were now on a first name basis. "Julia, would you like to relax in the living room?"

"Of course, Devon," she gushed, "This wine is superb. I think I'm getting just a bit loopy. Maybe I shouldn't imbibe anymore."

"Nonsense," Dad responded, "I have this shipped in from France. If you're worried about driving home, perhaps we can make other arrangements?"

"Oh Devon," she giggled, "Okay, you've talked me into it. My honor lies in your hands."

Fucking A!

I re-filled each of their wine goblets with more of the potent French wine which as just a drop more of the Liquid-X, and sent them off to the living room.

CHAPTER 5

An hour later I tiptoed down the main staircase, and poked my head around to peek inside our huge living room. My jaw almost dropped to the floor at what I saw.

Dad and Ms. Henderson were both passed out on the couch. Both fully clothed; Ms. Henderson snoring loudly.

Oh Good Lord!

I ran back upstairs to my room and quickly phoned Shelly. "What the hell, Shelly? What kind of Liquid-X did you give me? They're both passed out in the living room. I thought it was supposed to make them unbearably horny? They are still fully dressed, snoozing away!"

"Hey," Shelly snapped, "This stuff is made in some dude's basement. There's no guarantee it's gonna have the same effect as the pure stuff, what the hell?"

I was frustrated, but in all honesty, I couldn't blame Shelly for getting some homegrown Liquid-X last minute. "Sorry," I replied, "I'm just so disappointed is all."

"Well, it was a bad plan anyway," my friend remarked, "Better come up with another one."

I went back downstairs and finished loading the dishwasher. There was some wine left in the bottle, so I poured myself a glass, and just for shits and giggles, I put a few drops of the generic Liquid-X in it. If nothing else, I'd get a good night's sleep out of it.

***

My eyes opened to darkness. I was groggy as hell, having no clue as to how I got up to my bedroom. The last thing I recalled was finishing up in the kitchen, checking on Dad and Ms. Henderson who were still sawing logs.

And then what?

My eyelids felt as if they weighed a ton. I groggily reached over to find my bedside lamp, feeling around for it when I realized I wasn't in my room.

My eyes adjusted to the darkness, and I could see light streaming from beneath the closed bathroom door. Bloody hell! I was in Devon's bed. What the hell?

How did I get in here?

I felt around the bed, my desperately trying to get my bleary eyes adjusted to the darkness of Devon's room.

Just then the bathroom door opened, casting more light into his suite. He approached the bed, and as I quickly tried to sit up, my eyes widened at his nakedness.

"Wh-what happened?" I asked as he gazed down at me, his eyes looking at me like a wild animal assessing his prey. It was a look that was foreign to me, and my blood ran cold.

"I think you know damn well what happened Taylor," he said huskily. "You attempted to roofie me and your teacher, what the hell were you trying to accomplish with that stunt?"

Clearly, he was angry.

"I found that little vial you left in the kitchen. I'm not a fool, little girl. Would you care to explain?"

I fumbled for words. Confusion still wracking my brain. "But . . . but how did I get here? In your bed, I mean?" I asked, swallowing hard.

And at that moment, I felt my nakedness under the sheets, I lifted the top one, and peeked to make sure I wasn't hallucinating.

Nope, I was naked except for my panties. "Did you----?" I left the question hanging between us. I guess that Liquid-X had done a number on me as well, although not what I'd expected.

"What? Did I fuck you?" he asked, a smirk crossing his beautiful mouth. "Not yet. I prefer my partners not be comatose when I fuck them. I'm waiting for an answer Taylor as to what the hell you were thinking."

I felt a shiver go up my spine, and then some defiance kicked in. "I found those pictures you took of me. I also found several of my silk panties in the same box on your closet shelf.

Don't you think you owe me some explanation, *Dad*?" I quipped, a hint of belligerence lacing my words.

But he didn't flinch. He didn't appear ashamed or apologetic that he'd been busted. So, in a way, I guess we'd both been busted.

"I'm waiting for an explanation," he said, his voice stern as he watched me.

I exhaled a hard breath. "Okay, here it is. I'm so tired of you keeping such a tight rein on me. I'm a woman. I'm over eighteen, but you don't seem to realize that. You are way too protective and . . . strict with your rules. It's not fair. I feel like you're obsessed with keeping me a virgin, and for what?" I snapped, my anger now visible. "I want to date like normal eighteen year-olds. I want to experience relationships. What reason do you have for not allowing me to experience life, love and lust? What are you saving me for?"

"That's easy," he replied, his voice thick with desire. "For me."

His intentions were clear.

"Ohhh no. This can't possibly happen," I announced, gathering my courage and leaping out of his bed.

I ran downstairs to the kitchen, my breath coming in pants. The truth was, I wanted it to happen. Just now, seeing Devon as the virile and handsome man he was, had stirred something inside the woman in me. We were not blood. I knew he loved me and I loved him - but not in the way lovers loved one another.

But it felt wrong. Wrong to Mom. Wrong in every way possible.

I grabbed a bottled water from the fridge and took a long draw from it. I felt his presence in the room.

He was standing there, stark naked, rubbing his hand on the back of his neck as if needed to search for his words. "I'm sorry, Taylor. I had no right to invade your privacy, but I would be lying if I said I didn't crave you in every way a man craves a woman. Maybe I am too damn protective, but I want to be the one who takes your virginity. I want your first time to be the best. I want you to compare whomever comes after me with your first time with me."

And in that moment, I knew he wanted the same damn thing I wanted. He was waiting for my response, for permission to be the one to deflower me. And the truth was, I couldn't think of a better man to accomplish that task. Mom was gone. There was no judgment around. And I knew Devon would make the experience beautiful . . . because he did love me as a woman.

"Do it," I dared.

He closed the distance, pulling me up against him, his tongue ravaged my lips, parting them and swirling against mine, his teeth nipped at my lower lip, tugging and pulling until I moaned softly.

His hands were cupping my face so that I couldn't move away—not that I wanted to.

Being locked against him in this frenzied and passionate embrace was suddenly my own self-proclaimed heaven.

I molded myself to him provocatively, grinding my pelvis against his crotch.

He broke the kiss to stand back and gaze at my body. My eyes were fixed on the firm, hard expanse of his well-muscled chest and shoulders.

With his gaze lingering on every inch of my heaving breasts, I watched, totally mesmerized as his hands made their way to the under-swell of my tits.

He cupped them almost possessively, he ran his thumbs across my erect nipples, groaning in the process, showing his appreciation. I'd never felt anything so exciting in my life!

I melted into him and the next thing I'm aware of was being in his arms as he placed me gently on the cold, hardwood kitchen table.

His breathing was heavy and his intent was clear. He spread my legs, and I could clearly see in his bright, glazed over eyes that he wanted me and only me. I could feel his need, branding me like a hot iron, making its mark—his mark. His claim.

I leaned back on my arms, my gaze never wavered from his gorgeous face as I lifted my hips, my body language begged for him to relieve me of my panties.

That simple gesture was all it took for him to rip my silk panties from my body in a heated need to see my virgin pussy up close and personal.

I sat completely naked before him, panting like I'd just run a marathon. Placing both of his large, calloused hands on either side of my thighs, Devon dropped to his knees and began feasting on my pussy like a starved man.

I felt the hitch in my breath at the first contact of his mouth on my clit, rolling it with his tongue and sucking it tightly between his lips.

Fuck!

I moaned; he groaned.

Our eyes met before he leaned back for just a fraction of a second, licking my wetness from his swollen lips. "You taste even better than her."

And that made me happier than I ever thought possible. Biting on my bottom lip and staring at him through my hooded eyes, I pushed my hips upward toward his mouth, wanting him to continue, begging him to help me get to that release that I knew he could give me.

Devon was a virtuoso at eating pussy. How I knew that, I wasn't sure, but there was no doubt in my mind that without a doubt, he had spoiled me for anyone else.

Ever.

"God, Dad . . . please don't stop!" I could barely recognize my own voice and I realized that he alone had made me a woman this night. He alone had wrecked me for any other male on this earth. It was primal and it was meant to be because the chemistry was just that epic between the two of us.

He reached down and lifted my legs up and around, hooking them around his neck. "Call me Devon," he growled, "That's the only way this can work," and the next thing I knew he was burying his mouth once again over my drenched pussy.

Holy shit!

Letting my head fall back on the table, I groaned when I felt the thump against the hard surface. Between the heavenly feeling between my legs, the sound of our lust echoing off the walls and the scent of our combined sexual tension enveloping us in our own private cocoon, I could feel myself drifting into another sphere.

That's when I felt his thick finger slide inside of me as his tongue circled my clit, making me scream from surprise and from pleasure.

The wet, slick sounds coming from my pussy should have been embarrassing me because I wasn't sure if that was normal, but any concern was quickly being replaced with pure arousal and mounting pleasure.

Something was happening. Something that sure as hell hadn't happened before when I brought myself to orgasm thrumming my clit.

Way stronger.

Way deeper.

"Oh my God!" I shrieked. "Da—Devon, what's . . . what's happening?" My breathing was coming much quicker, just like my heartbeats.

"It's all good, Taylor," he crooned "Let it come, baby."

Snaking his free hand under my ass, Devon pushed his finger deeper inside of me and then turned it, thrusting so deeply I swore he was hitting my womb!

Then, it was like he had somehow hit the detonator of some massive orgasm that I didn't know existed—and maybe it *didn't* exist for anyone else but us, but I couldn't help but scream his name as powerful waves of pleasure exploded, one right after the other, penetrating every nerve ending, muscle and cell of my body.

Trembling, I felt his finger sliding out of me as his tongue was thoroughly lapping up every drop of this liquid release of mine. Spasms were still rocking my body as I slowly came down from the most beautiful and mind-fucking-boggling experience of my life.

Devon didn't stop. His mouth was lingering over my skin, leaving a trail of goose bumps as he peppered open-mouthed kisses up the length of my stomach.

"Oh, Devon . . ." I couldn't help the breathy quality of my voice, feeling as though every one of my dreams had come true.

Through the hazy fuck-fog of my rattled brain, I heard the distinct moans he emitted as his mouth re-visited my breasts, his tongue circling one nipple and then moving to the other. His teeth nipped and pulled until he suckled my left breast, nursing it like it belonged to him and only him.

"Baby," he rasped, his hand now gripping his huge erection that had slapped against his abdomen, "Tell me how much you want my cock inside of you."

"God, Devon yes! I want you to break my cherry. I want you to fuck me like your life depends on it!"

"Fuck, I want to be inside of you. Tell me you want this. Beg me, Taylor." His voice was rough, almost pleading, yet edged with a raw quality that made me want to come all over again.

"Yes, God yes. Please Devon, please, I'm begging you. Fuck me. Do it now!"

That's when I heard a growl, a fucking growl like a caveman taking what was clearly his. Pulling me closer to him, he stood straight and proud, watching me as he ran his tongue across his glistening lips.

Inching the bulbous head of his cock into my slick entrance, he leaned down and captured my lips with his own. His tongue teased mine, and he nipped at my lower lip with his teeth, taking my mind off of the girth he was slowly inching into me.

His fullness pressed deeper, and a flash of white pain suffused my core causing me to cry out against his mouth that was claiming me at the moment.

He released a masculine groan as he pushed himself in deeper. I heard a muffled curse and then he spoke more clearly. "Damn it if you're pussy isn't the tightest one I've ever had," he rasped.

And then he gave it to me full force, backing out, and then slamming his cock back into me, causing me to cry out again, and then mewl with the aftershocks of it.

"Sorry, baby," he said soothingly, "it can't be helped. Stay with me." The pain lasted for a couple of more thrusts and then my sex did what it was supposed to do: it welcomed him. I was so damn wet for him now, that I wasn't sure how much of the wetness was blood, and how much was lubrication.

I wrapped my legs around his hips tightly. My feet were planted firmly on his muscular ass, and my toes were digging in to grip and rock him into me deeper. I needed him in all the way.

My body was begging for him to be fully encased within me. He moaned, softly, licking my ear, his warm breath caressing my neck as he moaned again, thrusting a bit deeper.

"God baby, this is mine, do you get that? I want my dick buried inside of you all night long."

And his words made me wetter still as I felt myself clenching his shaft, adjusting to his girth. "I want that too."

He moved deeper yet inside of me and I moved my legs higher to his lower back, drawing him in deeper.

"That's it baby," he crooned as he started moving rhythmically within me, slowly and sensually, filling my core with his manhood. "So fucking tight. You doing okay?"

"Yes, Devon," I replied softly moving against him.

"Okay, cause I'm gonna start fucking you a little faster. But baby, you have to let me know if it hurts, and I promise I'll stop."

"Okay."

And his thrusting became a bit faster and deeper, his hips moving deliciously so that the head of his cock was hitting that special spot deep inside of me that his fingers had just recently brought to a pulsating orgasm. My first ever—that way.

He backed out and slammed in again, faster, harder deeper and I moaned his name over and over again. His mouth had lowered to mine and his tongue mated with my tongue as his cock was pleasuring my pussy in ways I never dreamed possible.

"Ahh, that's it baby," he crooned as my hips bucked up against him and my moans became feral as every primal instinct in me responded to his mating.

And I knew at that moment that his cock was truly mine. I knew that no other man could ever make me feel the way that he was making me feel at this moment.

I arched my back and deep within my core the slow, deliberate warmth was starting and spreading through every nerve ending and muscle in my body.

I felt my heat gripping him, pulling him and he groaned loudly as he joined me in the same spiraling vortex of pleasure that our joined bodies had created.

"God, Taylor, I'm coming," he groaned, pounding into me with lustful force, my moans now getting louder and words couldn't even form on my lips as our orgasms washed over each of us.

I was aware of the sounds and the scents: skin slapping skin; our wet juices mingling together and it was potent to every sense we possessed.

Devon stilled and I could feel the throbbing of his cock inside of me as he emptied his seed into my fertile womb, over and over until with one final shudder, he finished.

Our breathing was slowing down and our senses slowly returned with a peaceful calm in the afterglow of our climactic coupling.

Devon leaned over again, and brushed soft kisses on my cheeks, nose and chin; his tongue traced my lower lip slowly as his sapphire eyes gazed into mine with a dark depth that was new to me. He lowered his eyelids and his dark eyelashes looked like sooty fringe against his skin.

"Are you going to be my good girl from here on out?" he asked huskily. "No more roofies?"

I smiled, "I promise, Dad, I mean *Devon*. Sorry! This is a little difficult to get used to for me. But I don't regret one second of it. After all, you are the only man in my life who loves me and who I truly love, but . . . "

"Go on," he said huskily, "But *what*?"

"But what will it take for you to extend my curfew on the weekends to say, oh one a.m.?"

He was thoughtful for a moment. "I think we can work something out. But I'll have to approve of whomever it is you want to spend time with. I warn you little girl, I can be extremely protective when it comes to you. I think you and I need to practice giving and taking. How does that sound?"

I leaned in my tongue traced his bottom lip. "Sounds good to me. By the way, how did Ms. Henderson get home?" I teased.

"She didn't," he replied with an ornery grin. "I carried her up and put her in your bed. I'm thinking I might want to fuck her once I wash your blood and cum off of my cock. Do you wanna watch?"

I squealed in delight. "Yes, Devon! Promise me you'll fuck an "A" out of her for my upcoming quarter grade in English, will you?"

He smirked, giving my bare ass a playful smack. "I'll do my best little girl."

THE END

Other Books by Willa Winters

BECAUSE OF YOU

SYNOPSIS:

Lexi Connors-Nettleman has led a charmed life. Her father died when Lexi was only two years old, leaving her and her mother a hefty insurance policy. Sadly, Lexi's mother blew through the money in a matter of months, and with no employable skills, she did the next best thing: she married money.

Marion Connors married Archibald (Archie) Nettleman when Lexi was three years old. Archie was thirty years older than her mother, and though he raised Lexi as his own, as she got older, people they didn't know often mistook him for her grandfather instead of her daddy. That's right, Archie legally adopted Lexi when she reached the tender age of seven.

Life for the Nettlemans was comfortable and privileged. When Lexi was fourteen, she was sent away to an exclusive girls boarding school in Switzerland. At eighteen she graduated and anxiously flew back home to be with her parents in Naples, Florida.

But when she arrived back at the sprawling mansion near the beach, she received the shock of her life. Her mother had taken off with the pool boy three months prior, and Archie was fit to be tied!

Lexi clearly had walked into a situation, at barely eighteen, she was ill-equipped to handle!

TEASER FOR BECAUSE OF YOU

The Discovery

The limousine pulled up the circular drive and stopped in front of the huge double doors of the mansion. I was surprised that neither Mom nor Daddy had made the trip to Miami to welcome me back home. The flight from Geneva to Miami had worn me out, despite the fact I'd flown first class as always. But it seemed strange to me that neither one of them had been there to greet me.

When I had descended to the terminal on an escalator, I immediately spotted a limo driver holding up a sign that read: Lexi Connors-Nettleman.

I hadn't been home for a visit in two years, and my mother's calls had stopped weeks ago. I hadn't been all that concerned because I knew my mother was always busy with charity luncheons, planning fundraising events, volunteering for outreach programs, bridge club, and of course her favorite hobby: shopping for couture.

At forty, my mother still managed to spend as much time as possible on the go, away from Archie. I had figured out a long time ago that their marriage was built on two fundamental things: money (for my mother) and sex (for Archie). I knew sure as shit the money would never get old as far as Mom was concerned, but Archie--er, Daddy I meant, well he, was seventy years old! Could old men still, you know, *do it?*

The driver opened the door and helped me out. He emptied the trunk of all of my luggage, and followed me up the steps to the mammoth, pillared front porch. I no sooner reached the door when it was flung open, and our maid, Lucy, was pulling me in for a hug. "So glad you're home, Lexi," she said, "We've missed you around here, that's for sure, *mon petite*!"

Lucy was more than a maid. She'd always been like a second mom to me. She was a few years older than Mom. She was of Cajun ethnicity, her creamy olive skin, dark hair and eyes gave her an exotic look, but she was totally down to earth, if not sometimes outspoken when it came to issues involving me.

She often threw a few French phrases into her dialogue, which I thought was totally classy. I thought of her as a protector of sorts. I knew she and Mom didn't get on well. In fact, Mom had wanted her fired more than once, but it was a battle she lost with Daddy. Lucy had been with Daddy since before we came into his life.

"Come, come in, your papa is not here at the moment, but I expect him for dinner. You must be so tired after your long trip!"

She stopped her fussing over me just long enough to instruct the driver where to place my luggage and then turned her attention back to me as he departed. "Are you hungry?"

"Lucy," I interrupted, "Where's Mom? Is she with Daddy?"

Her expression went void. She didn't respond to my question right away, wringing her hands. It was seldom that Lucy was at a loss for words, but clearly that was the case at the moment.

"What's wrong?" I pressed, "Tell me."

"Oh *mon cherie*," she said, her voice tentative, "It should be your papa to tell you this, dammit. Your mere, she left several months ago. She has left your father."

"What?" I screamed, "Why, where--?"

Lucy was visibly shaken. She stepped close to me; her hands braced each of my shoulders as she locked her dark eyes with my blue ones.

"Your mama, well she left with Juan Gutierrez. They are in love."

"Juan...*Juan the pool guy*?" I shrieked in total disbelief.

"Oui mon tendre," she replied. Lucy didn't generally toss out so much French unless she was angry or emotional. I knew she wasn't angry at me.

"But why?" I asked, "Why would she do that without telling me or letting me know? Do you even know where they are living?"

"No, I'm sorry, Lexi. I don't know and I don't care. She never should have done this to you."

"How does Daddy feel about it?" I asked carefully. I knew that the relationship between Daddy and Mom had deteriorated when I visited from school two years ago. It was one of the reasons I chose not to go home for the summer last year. They no longer shared a bedroom, and I could feel the frostiness every time they were in the same room together.

"Your papa, he's adjusted. Come, let me help you unpack. You can discuss this in detail when your papa gets home."

After Lucy helped me unpack, I told her I was going to take a nap. It was four in the afternoon, but I seriously was jet-lagged, and the emotional shock I received upon my return had drained what little energy I had left.

I tried to nap, but thoughts, questions and lingering doubts kept playing in my head.

I knew my mother had been self-centered and frivolous, but that was how she'd *always* been. Daddy knew that when he married her. What had changed? Did the age difference suddenly become an obstacle for her? Had the sex been bad? As I thought back, they never exhibited much affection, at least not in public or in front of me. I mean, I used to sometimes hear things behind their bedroom door. Strange noises I couldn't place. Moans, slapping, and sometimes, the sounds of snapping leather...like a belt being used.

I'd never asked her about it, because whatever it was, it didn't seem to bother my mother. She always seemed perfectly fine the next day. Chipper as always, and off to another shopping spree with Daddy's credit cards. I figured that was just how married people behaved. What did I know?

I was eighteen and had been squirreled away at a private girl's academy for the past four years. I had no point of reference on relationships at all. For all I knew, my mother and father's marriage was typical. Now I had my doubts.

The pool guy?

How cliché was that?

When sleep refused to come, I got up from my bed, showered and dressed for dinner. I had to face Daddy soon, and I was anxious to hear his side of the story, and more than that, what would be in store for me going forward.

END OF TEASER

AVAILABLE NOW!

BECAUSE OF US

SYNOPSIS:

Nineteen year-old Christina is a hot mess!

Kicked out of college for aberrant behavior, she must now face her mother and stepfather when she makes the ***trip of shame*** back home. Wild and willful, she has no intention of being reined in.

Jonah Mitchell has raised Christina since she was ten years-old. She had been his princess, but now he realizes that Christina requires a firmer hand. And who better to administer the needed discipline than he?

When they face off, things get pretty *sticky.* This taboo short story romance will satisfy the kink in all of us!

ADULT CONTENT

BECAUSE OF US TEASER

I tried to slip into the house quietly. I knew I had to face my mom and stepdad eventually, but not tonight. I'd been through so much today what with packing up all my shit, and driving the four and a half drive from my college dorm to our house in Franklin, Idaho.

I wasn't in the mood for an hour long lecture about how I'd screwed things up at college, wasted their money, and could kiss my scholarship goodbye since I'd been expelled for behavioral and academic violations.

It sounded so much worse than it really was!

So, I plagiarized a term paper, big deal. And so I got caught fucking one of my professors in return for giving me a passing grade.

It didn't help that we were fucking like animals on the top of his desk when the Dean of Students walked in just as we were reaching mutual satisfaction so to speak.

I'm sure the university had given my parents the whole lurid story not holding back any details.

My stepdad had called me on my cell, and being that he'd raised me for the past ten years, since I was a freckled faced ten year old, I knew by the tone in his voice he was more than agitated, he was furious!

"Get your ass home immediately, Christina," he'd growled over the phone. "Your mother and I will deal with you once you're back here. Let me warn you now, we won't be tolerating this type of behavior as long as you're under our roof. If you can't handle school, then I'll put you to work at the garage. Maybe if you get your hands good and dirty you'll learn to appreciate the education you so flagrantly tossed away."

And then he'd hung up on me.

Just like that.

Daddy--that's what I'd called him from the beginning since I'd never known my biological father, had rarely been that angry with me. I'd always been his princess.

Now things would be different.

His princess had fallen from grace in a big way. Apparently, my mom had been too angry to even talk to me.

Of course, Mom's anger was way different than Dad's. She tended to internalize stuff, blaming herself for not doing enough, or doing too much. She'd always left the disciplinary action to him.

Christ, I wondered if I had a spanking coming?

I stifled a soft giggle as I let myself into the house with my key. It was nearly midnight, so I knew they'd be in bed. At least I could get a good night's sleep before I had to face their wrath in the morning. Right now, I didn't have the energy.

I crept up the carpeted steps thankful there were no creaky spots. As I walked down the hallway towards the door of their room, I could see they'd left it partially open which they never did unless they were waiting for me to get home.

As a teenager, they'd watched every move I made. Dad, in particular, was protective and strict with curfews, interrogating the boys I dated, and grounding my ass for any menial infraction of his rules. He always said he wasn't raising a slut.

Guess he was wrong about that.

As I tiptoed, holding my breath, noises coming from their room caused me to stop in my tracks.

Oh. My. God.

My parents were having sex! I recognized the sounds of skin slapping skin, soft moans, and the heavy breathing of sexual play going on in their darkened room.

END OF TEASER

AVAILABLE NOW!

BECAUSE OF HIM

SYNOPSIS:

Why would I ever want Tyrone out of my life?

My stepfather, Tyrone, entered my life when I was two years old. He was the only man I called Daddy--if not by blood, certainly by love. He and Mom gave me a little brother, Sly, who I adored.

Dad always treated me as if I were his blood child. Sly and I had been blessed with a wonderful father. He was a corporate lawyer, but had always found the time to attend our sporting events, take us camping, and dry our tears when necessary. Just because our mom had kicked him to the curb, didn't mean I was going to - he was the only dad I'd ever known.

When I turned eighteen, he bought me a brand new car as promised, and sent me off to college paying my tuition as well. I never knew the extent of his love for me, but when I came home for winter break during my freshman year at college, with my new boyfriend in tow, I was about to find out!

This taboo short read is chock full of forbidden taboo and romance. If you like the stepfather romance genre, you're gonna adore this one! The interracial aspect makes it even hotter!

ADULT CONTENT

BECAUSE OF HIM TEASER

"Hush, baby girl," he crooned. "I know I lost it with you. It's just . . . you've never gone against my rules before Danielle. You've always respected me and the rules of my house. I was, I don't know, *shocked* to see what you were doing under my roof with that idiot," he finished with a growl.

His hands were soothing me. He continued to massage my back, and slowly, I felt his hand move a bit lower to just above the swell of my ass. "Hey, are you going to talk to me?" he asked gently.

I was too ashamed to pull my face out of the pillow. I shook my head, another sob escaped.

"Oh baby girl," he said softly, "Don't you understand that sex is a beautiful thing under the right circumstances? I know you're a woman now. A very bright, beautiful and sexy woman at that."

His palm moved lower yet, his caresses were stirring something deep inside of me. Something totally unfamiliar.

His deep, rich voice continued. "It's not that I expect you to deny yourself of your carnal instincts, but I don't think you should force them either as some means of proving you're gay or not gay. Does that make sense?"

The truth was that it made *perfect* sense. I understood the point he was trying to get across to me. I nodded.

He continued talking to me. "It wasn't but a few weeks back when I called and you opened up to me about how upset you were with this guy. You questioned your own sexuality. I told you then and I'm telling you now that you need to stop worrying about it. Allow things to happen naturally as they should. There's an old song that comes to mind; something about 'you can't hurry love, you just have to wait.' Don't rush things that you're not sure you really want, okay?"

I nodded again, sniffling. His words were intended to guide me, to affect the decision making process, but right now, his warm strong hand that was massaging my ass was affecting me more than anything.

Yes, it was affecting me as a man affects a woman; as the touch of a lover is supposed to arouse his or her mate. His touch affected me way more than Brandon's touch had. In fact, it wasn't even close.

My pussy was getting wet again. I was positive he had not intended to have such an effect on his little girl.

END OF TEASER

BECAUSE OF THEM

SYNOPSIS:

What a girl won't do for a college education!

Twenty year-old Sherry Monroe is struggling to meet her college tuition. She has no social life, and on top of that, she's got no place to go during spring break. So while all of her friends are soaking up the sun on pristine beaches from Florida to California, Sherry is in Carbondale playing marriage counselor to her mother.

Sometimes a kind heart can become a heart of stone when lust and betrayal enter the equation.

BECAUSE OF THEM TEASER

I'd only been home for a day and a night when I could no longer pretend that the tension between my mother and James wasn't there.

Mama hadn't been very talkative to me since my arrival, which was odd since there wasn't anything I could've done to piss her off. James had just been quiet and withdrawn. It was unusual behavior for the both of them, and it unnerved me to say the least.

I was in my room, folding clean laundry on my bed. I'd saved about two weeks' worth of dirty laundry to bring home to do, but I knew Mama wasn't pissed about that because it was fairly common for me to do that to save money. There was a soft tap on my door.

"Come in," I called out, figuring it was Mama.

It was James. And his expression said it was something serious.

"Got a couple of minutes, Cupcake?"

I smiled and nodded. "Are you ever going to call me by my real name?" I asked, as I folded up a pair of jeans.

He closed the door softly behind him, and sat down on the bed. "I'm sorry, Sherry, you know, old habits die hard. For this discussion, I think I'd best call you by your name. So, do you have a few minutes to talk, *Sherry Darling?*"

He put extra emphasis on my name the second time around. He had called me *Sherry Darling* and *Cupcake* the whole time I was growing up. At my current age, I certainly preferred Sherry Darling over Cupcake!

"Sure," I said, biting my lower lip. God I hope it wasn't bad news. I said a silent prayer that it wouldn't be.

He paused for a moment and I studied him. His thick dark hair was just above the collar of his shirt. I loved how disheveled it looked. It made him look even more rugged and sexy in my opinion. His intense blue eyes seemed even bluer as he searched his thoughts for his opening line. His hesitation didn't serve to assuage my nerves at all.

"Sherry," he said, and I loved the way my name sounded on his lips, "your mom and I well–you know we've been trying to get pregnant for a while now. We've spent a shitload of money on fertility testing, treatments—the whole shebang. Now I know this isn't news to you, because unfortunately, all of it has put us in a financial position where we haven't been able to help you the way we wanted to with your college and all. And for that, I'm really, really sorry."

Oh shit.

"You want me to leave school," I interrupted, knowing full well that's what he was trying to get out there. And if that were the case, I know I wouldn't have any choice in the matter. I'd have to be an adult about it, and not show just how much that would mess up my plans for the future.

"No, honey. No—that's not it. It's a bit more… *complicated* than that, and I have to warn you right now, it's so damn difficult for me to even ask it of you, but your mother just couldn't bring herself to do it."

Now I was totally scared. "Is Mama okay?" God, what would I do if he was about to tell me that during all of the testing the doctors had performed, they found something wrong with her. Something that was terminal and now my stepfather was forced to deliver the bad news to me. I swallowed nervously.

"Oh no, baby," he replied, shaking his head back and forth. "I'm sorry I'm fumbling around with this. She's fine, but you see, we found out that there's no way she can conceive a baby. And it's pretty much devastated her. That's where we kind of need your help, and why this is so damn difficult. God, we will totally understand if you refuse us, and we won't love you any less. I want you to know that right off the bat, okay?"

I swallowed again. I was more nervous now than I had been before. But I nodded my head indicating for him to continue. I had a sinking feeling that my stepfather was about to drop a major bomb on me.

"Here's the thing, darlin', you see, we don't have the money to pay for a surrogate to carry our baby. Hell, we don't have the money for artificial insemination even. So, what your mother and I are proposing is making you an offer."

"An... offer?"

"Yes–an *offer.* If you carry the baby...and be our surrogate so to speak, we can afford to pay for your tuition—even if it means we take out loans to do it, and of course, you're covered under our medical insurance for all costs associated with the prenatal and birthing expenses."

Oh my God! I had never expected that this was what he needed to discuss with me. How could they possibly ask this of me?

AVAILABLE NOW!

BECAUSE OF HER

SYNOPSIS

The bigger the cushion, the sweeter the pushin!

Becca was about to graduate college. As an only child, she had always been the object of her mother's overbearing and critical remarks regarding her weight. She'd even sent her to fat farms as a child.

Becca found college a blessed escape from her perfectionist mother. She was happy to finally be distanced and estranged from those painful memories of her formative years.

Just when Becca thought she was home-free, out of the blue her mother contacts her with the news she was getting married. She insisted Becca come home to greet her new *stepdaddy*, Buck, and wanted to mend fences.

How could Becca refuse the olive branch her mother extended? But little did she know exactly what awaited her at the other end of that olive branch.

ADULT CONTENT

BECAUSE OF HER TEASER

I was home.

I'd been home for a week and it hadn't taken Mom more than twenty-four hours to put me on a protein diet. What she didn't know was that I'd come back to Charlotte well-stocked with my favorite guilty pleasures!

Snickers, Reese Cups, Twizzlers, and Butterfingers made up most of my stash. And I kept them well hidden. My mother wasn't above search and seizure, no matter how old I was.

She was a control freak, and nothing would deter her once she set her mind to achieving some inane goal. Such as making me skinny.

Now that Mom was engaged to a millionaire, her mission was to focus on improving her social status, and dragging me along with her.

"You know Buck's been a widow for eighteen years. I'm the first woman he's loved since his dearly- departed wife. They were married for thirty years. I swear his penthouse has one room that is practically a shrine to her," she said, her tone definitely agitated by this. "Once we're married, that will change let me assure you."

"I'm certain it will," I replied distractedly. I was on my laptop, searching Indeed.com for at least an entry level job, be it part-time or full-time to start generating some income.

"What's that supposed to mean?" she snapped, looking over at me from where she was lounging on a chaise, buffing her nails.

I shrugged. "I just know that if something bugs you like that, you'll figure out a way to get rid of it."

"Well! Thanks so much for clarifying that, sweetheart. You make me sound like a vicious bitch. I get that a man grieves when he loses his wife, but damn, it's been eighteen years!"

"I'm sure he'll understand, Mom," I said, clicking a link to upload my updated resume. "Did they have children?" I asked.

She stopped filing her nails. "Oh God," she said excitedly, "That's what I've been meaning to tell you. Buck is in San Antonio now visiting his son, Jake. Apparently, Jake has just gone through a nasty divorce. Buck is trying to convince him to relocate to Charlotte. From what I've heard from Buck, Jake is quite a catch. He's thirty-one, a graduate of the University of Texas with a Master's Degree in Marketing. He'd be a great addition to the company. And," she continued with a huge smile on her face, "Who knows, he just might be a great catch for my little girl." She gave me a salacious wink.

"Mom," I said using my strict voice, "Don't start any matchmaking. My plate is full. I have my own priorities going on, okay?" I continued tapping away on my laptop.

She scoffed. "That's your problem, Becca. Full plates have been your priority. Now you get yourself in shape, and you will have men falling at your feet, trust me," she finished with a snicker. "I don't have to work anymore. Buck wants me to live a life of leisure, and I want you to have the same options. He wants more children," she scoffed. "I never told him I had my tubes tied. I'll keep that to myself and just tell him it's harder to conceive past forty. What the heck are you doing on your computer over there?" she asked.

"I'm putting out my resumes, Mom. I need to get a job."

She got up from the chaise, and came over standing behind my chair, looking over my shoulder. "Nonsense, honey. Why you can do much better than that. Why don't you ask your soon-to-be stepdaddy if he can use you at the company? It would be a real boon to that resume of yours."

I swiveled around in my chair looking up at her. "Mom, I said patiently, "I like doing things on my own. I don't want to use your relationship with Buck to carve out my career. I'm perfectly willing and capable of doing this all by myself."

She leaned down so that our eyes were level. "Listen to me," she said succinctly, "Do you think I'm marrying a seventy-two year old saggy balled coot for my health? I'm doing this as much for you as I am for myself. Now I've worked hard ever since your daddy died, haven't I?"

I nodded, totally blown away by the words she was spewing to me in confidence right now. For the first time in what seemed like forever, my mother had removed her mask and was exposing herself for what she knew she was, and for some odd reason, I had a little bit of respect for that.

"And I know along the way, I kissed a lot of frogs, and pity-fucked men who I thought might be an alternative for you being fatherless and all. None of them panned out as you well know. But this time--this time Becca I'm doing what I need to do so that I leave you with more than I ever could have on my own. So please, I'm asking you to put aside your pride and let your mama do what she can to make up for my shortcomings in the past. Will you do that?"

END OF TEASER

About The Author

Willa Winters is a pseudonym for a best-selling author who doesn't want to horrify her friends, family and readers with the super-kink flavor of her *Scandalous Series.*

Do you enjoy lusty tales of depravity? Don't feel bad. Everyone needs to get their kink on! So, pour yourself a glass of wine, relax and take the deep dive into these scandalous books. Remember: ***It's just fiction.***

You can check out my backlist here!

Willa Winters Backlist

Made in the USA
Monee, IL
12 June 2024

59838347R00069